THE ODD POTATO

• A CHANUKAH STORY •

BY EILEEN BLUESTONE SHERMAN
Illustrated by Katherine Janus Kahn

KAR-BEN COPIES • ROCKVILLE, MD

Library of Congress Cataloging in Publication Data

Sherman, Eileen Bluestone.
  The odd potato.

  Summary: Rachel turns an odd potato into a symbol of Hanukkah joy.
  1. Children's stories, America. [1 Hanukkah—Fiction. 2. Jews—Fiction.
3. Family life—Fiction]
I. Kahn, Katherine, ill. II. Title.
PZ7.S545520d 1984   [E]   84-17186
ISBN 0-930494-36-9
ISBN 0-930494-37-7 (pbk.)

Published by KAR-BEN COPIES, INC., Rockville, MD
Printed in the United States of America

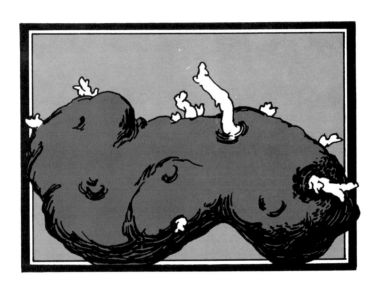

To My Parents,
Herman and Rita Bluestone

—E.B.S.

$\mathcal{R}$achel looked everywhere for the
Chanukah menorah.

When she asked her Dad to help her find it, he just shrugged and mumbled something about the attic.

He had not been any help last year, either. Since his wife's death, a long 18 months ago, Mr. Levy had shown no interest in holidays. Their sparkle had been snuffed out by his sorrow. He still prayed at the synagogue, but celebrations were another story. Last Chanukah, Rachel and her brother Sammy had spent the week with their cousins in Minneapolis, but this year the Levy children would be at home.

Still, Rachel was not discouraged. She had saved enough money from her weekly allowance to buy gifts for her father and brother, along with dreidels and candles from the synagogue gift shop. Now her only problem was to locate the family menorah. Except for a dollar or two, her money was spent.

A new menorah was out of the question, and she didn't dare bother her father again about the old one. Rachel remembered how much her mother had loved that menorah. It was one of the few possessions Rachel's grandmother had brought with her to America. But if her father did not want to use it, he must have a good reason.

Rachel decided she would concentrate on making latkes instead. She watched carefully in Hebrew school when Mrs. Rosenblum showed the class how to make the batter. She remembered watching her mother follow the very same steps each Chanukah.

Those times had always been very special. Cooking was fun, but even better was listening to her mother tell wonderful stories about her own childhood.

Without fail, Sammy would ruin it by barging into the kitchen and demanding his turn to stir. The lovely calm would turn to chaos. It seemed that all Sammy had to do was look at the bowl, and batter splattered from ceiling to floor.

But Rachel's mother's latkes were always scrumptious. She was not certain her own potato pancakes could match up, but she was determined to try.

*T*he afternoon before the first night of Chanukah, Rachel stopped by Weintraub's grocery for a bag of potatoes, but she couldn't find a single one. The bin was empty. Rachel began to cry.

"Rachel!" exclaimed Mr. Weintraub. "Don't be silly. Who cries over potatoes? I'll have more tomorrow. Buy rice instead."

"You can't make latkes from rice, Mr. Weintraub," Rachel sobbed.

"You have a point," he agreed. "Wait here. I'll see what I can do." He disappeared into his back room.

Mr. Weintraub returned a minute later holding a very odd-looking potato.

"It isn't much," he admitted. "All of my shoppers kept throwing it back into the bin. It's not rotten. It just looks funny. I suppose one potato won't make a lot of latkes, but it's the best I can do. Take it with my compliments."

Rachel studied the curious potato for a moment and suddenly screamed with delight. "Oh, Mr. Weintraub! Thank you! Thank you! This is perfect. It's just right. Thank you a million times." As Rachel rushed out of the store, Mr. Weintraub just shook his head and smiled.

Sammy greeted his older sister as she walked through the door.

"Where have you been? What's in the bag?"

"I was at the grocer's to buy potatoes," she answered.

Sammy grinned and squealed, "Oh great! We'll make latkes—just like old times."

He grabbed the bag from his sister's hand, and the odd potato fell to the floor. Sammy made a face.

"Oh gross!" he exclaimed. "Cancel the latkes."

Rachel smiled. "Don't worry, kid. You're not eating latkes tonight. I'm saving this potato for something more important."

Sammy looked puzzled. "Oh yeah? What?"

"Come into the kitchen and you'll see."

Sammy followed Rachel to the sink and watched her carefully scrub and dry the mysterious potato. "So now what?" he asked. Rachel could no longer contain her excitement.

"Don't you see, Sammy? It's perfect. For some reason, Daddy doesn't want to use our beautiful menorah, and I don't have any money to buy a new one.

"Until this afternoon, I had completely given up on lighting candles, but when I saw this potato, I remembered a story Mommy used to tell me. She always said we were lucky to have such a beautiful Chanukah menorah. When her Daddy was a little boy, his family was so poor they couldn't afford a real one, so they used a potato to hold the candles."

Suddenly, Sammy understood. "Oh, neat. It's perfect!"

*T*hat evening, before the family sat down to dinner, Rachel quietly reminded her father that it was the first night of Chanukah. Mr. Levy smiled and said, "Yes, honey. I haven't forgotten. In fact, this afternoon I spoke to your Uncle Louis, and your Chanukah treat is all arranged. You and Sammy are flying to Minneapolis this weekend for a wonderful celebration."

"That's great!" Sammy piped up, "But we don't have to wait. Come into the kitchen. We've got a surprise for you."

Mr. Levy did not know what to expect, but when he saw the odd potato holding candles for the first night of Chanukah, tears filled his eyes. His voice trembled as he spoke, "Children, it's beautiful. Your mother would be very proud. Let us light the candles."

Together they chanted the blessings as Rachel lit the candles.

After dinner they played with the dreidels Rachel had bought and congratulated her on the presents she had chosen.

At bedtime, Rachel confessed to her father that she, too, would like a special Chanukah gift.

Mr. Levy smiled. "That seems only fair," he said. "Anything in particular?"

"Yes, Daddy. Please help me find our Chanukah menorah. The potato is nice, but it's not the same."

"You're right, Rachel," he said. "Tonight I realized how much I, too, miss Mommy's beautiful menorah. We'll look for it together in the morning."

The next night the family chanted the blessings for the second night of Chanukah.

Standing side-by-side were two, very beautiful menorahs.

ABOUT THE AUTHOR

Eileen Bluestone Sherman is a playwright and lyricist whose plays for children have been produced by The Coterie, Hallmark's highly-acclaimed Showcase Theatre in Kansas City. She received her B.A. from Finch College and her M.A. in Theatre Arts from SUNY Albany. She lives in Kansas with her husband Neal and two children, Jenny and Joshua.

ABOUT THE ILLUSTRATOR

Katherine Janus Kahn received the Golden Hugo Award at the 1975 Chicago International Film Festival for her illustrations for *A Wizard of Earthsea* by Ursula LeGuin. Her vivid drawings for *The Passover Parrot,* published last spring, have been widely praised. She has created artwork for books, magazines, newspapers, and television. She lives in Maryland with her husband David and son Bertie.